THE FIGURE

J. PATRICK LEMARR

Edited by
DANI J. CAILE

WRITE CROWD PUBLISHING

For B, with thanks for nights spent watching horror movies.

CONTENTS

THE FIGURE

Dawn Prescott had been a counselor at Camp Montclair Lake for two summers and yet, despite the rumors and ghost stories about the place locals had dubbed Camp Nightmare Lake, she hadn't met a single vampire, swamp creature, werewolf, or dime store Freddy Krueger wannabe. It had been a running joke for the past three weeks. Whenever one of her 12-year-old charges had a nightmare that woke the whole cabin, or some terrified newbie counselor swore they saw a machete-wielding killer watching from the other side of the lake, Dawn would explain how boring the real world was.

"I come to this dump every summer," she'd say. "Hell, before I was a counselor, I was a camper here. Every story you've ever heard about a killing or a Satanic ritual or some deformed kid drowning because his counselors were off somewhere having sex is all BS. The most exciting thing that's ever happened in this camp was when Sandy Kline puked on her birthday cake after sneaking shots with the camp troublemaker."

To be fair to Dawn, she believed that to be true before the 9-inch hunting blade pierced her heart and spilled blood down her lemon-yellow "Camp is for Caring" t-shirt. Three campers and two other counselors were already dead by then. Dawn had been jogging with her noise-canceling earbuds in when the shelter in place siren sounded. It would be the last mistake she would ever make.

THE FIGURE

The siren was still cutting through the cool night air like a hatchet when Andy Vale herded a half-dozen campers into the mess hall pantry. The other children in camp likely didn't know what was out there or how near death truly was. They hadn't seen The Figure. But Andy and his campers had. They had caught a glimpse of it down by the boathouse just after discovering the corpse of Tom Brannigan, the camp's founder and owner, pinned to a tree by a pitchfork.

Now, with the lives of six frightened children in his

hands, Andy was doing the only thing that made sense: locking them in the pantry.

"You've got to listen to me," he said, hoping his words were connecting through their sobs. "Whatever is out there can't get to you in here. The door locks from the outside and I'm taking the key. All you need to do is stay quiet until I come back for you."

"Don't leave us, Andy," Carl Hoff pleaded.

"Never," Andy said. "I'm coming back for you. But I need to find Petey or Victoria. They have keys to the office and—" He paused, unsure of whether he should tell the children about the gun locked in Mr. Brannigan's desk.

"But we're just kids," Amy Wendt argued.

"No," he said adamantly. "Kids can't paddle a canoe as fast as you did today, Amy. Or shoot an arrow as straight as Timothy. And they sure as hell can't tackle a counselor like we all saw Lizzy do yesterday. You might have been kids when you got here three weeks ago, but you're so much more than that now. You're warriors. And you'll take care of each other until I come back."

"I'm scared," Timothy admitted, his freckled face further spotted by tears.

"It's okay to be scared. Fear keeps us alive. It tells us when to run. It tells us when to fight. Or when to hide. We just can't let it keep us from running, fighting, or hiding when the time comes."

"So right now, we hide," Carl said.

"Only until I get back," Andy said, "and then we run. Hard and fast across the picnic grounds until we reach the Hitchens' farm."

"What if you don't come back?" Amy asked.

Andy hadn't considered that. The question shook him. He turned to the quiet boy in the group, an introvert named Henry Aster, whom the other campers had taken to calling Casper because of his ability to enter and leave a room with no one noticing. He'd been the hardest camper for Andy to get to know.

"Henry knows the way to the Hitchens' place," Andy said. "If I don't come for you, one of the other counselors will. You run like hell, you hear me? You get to the farm and you call the cops."

"We don't want you to die," Lizzy insisted, her sobs stretching the word "die" into three syllables.

"Then we're all on the same page," Andy said, giving them a wink. "Stay here. Stay safe. I promise you that, while I'm still kicking, I won't rest until I get you all out of here."

One by one, they nodded, wiping their tears away with their bony forearms.

"Keep the lights out and don't move around or talk," Andy instructed.

Once he had padlocked the door behind him, he realized that keeping the key on him endangered those children. So long as he had it, the killer could get his hands on it. Searching the kitchen, he found a ceramic jarred labeled flour and pushed the key down into the fine, white powder.

It had begun raining on his way back from the boathouse, but now it was storming like the world was ending and The Figure was killing campers and counselors to make sure of it. In the dark, quiet of the empty mess hall, Andy took a deep breath and plotted a route to Cabin 11—Victoria's cabin—where he hoped to find keys that would grant him access to Brannigan's pistol.

Careful not to be seen leaving the mess hall, he bolted for the bulletin board directly across the main path. From its cover, he shielded his eyes from the rain, trembled when thunder shook the ground, then made his way down the Red Path toward the easternmost part of the camp.

Each path was color-coded to keep campers from getting lost. From any centralized building—the mess hall, the infirmary, the craft lodge, the gym—a camper could simply follow a colored path back to their cabin. The Blue Path led to cabins 1-3, the Green to cabins 4-9, the Red Path to cabins 10-12 and the main office, and the Orange to Cabin 13, the boathouse, and the amphitheater.

Less than 500 feet down the Red Path, Andy heard the snap of a twig and spun on his heels, ready to fight or flee. When he saw Drew Jenkins and 4 soaked-to-the-skin campers, he did neither.

"Geez, Vale, you scared the hell out of me," Drew said. "Where are the others?"

Suddenly, a scenario flashed through Andy's mind: a vision of Drew and his campers accidentally leading The Figure to the children he had locked in the pantry.

"You're the only ones I've seen," he lied. "I'm looking for Victoria or Petey. I need to get into the office."

"Petey's dead, bro," Drew said quietly, hoping the children wouldn't hear. "Found him and Jess on the archery range. Something's out there. It—" He leaned into Andy's ear and whisper, "gutted them, bro. Like fuckin' fish."

"Stay off the path," Andy said. "Stick to the trees. Get to the Hitchens' place. They've got a phone."

"Bro, *I've* got a phone," Drew said, holding up his cell. "I gave Brannigan my burner so I could stay in touch with my girl. But this storm is killing reception. I can't get a single bar, bro."

"That farm is old," Andy said. "They've got a land line. I'm sure of it. Go. I'm gonna find the others."

"Don't be a hero, man," Drew said. "Come with us."

"No. I-I need to find Victoria."

Drew nodded solemnly.

"Good luck, bro. Watch your six."

"Yeah. You, too."

He watched them shrink back into the bushes, then turned back toward the Red Path, jogging as fast as he could without making more noise than the storm would cover. Every flash of lightning made him feel exposed. Every crash of thunder made him jump out of his skin.

By the time he approached Cabin 10, the rain was coming down harder than ever and the air had chilled to the point that Andy could see his breath. And then the scream chilled his spine faster than any storm ever could. Victoria's scream. Terror given voice.

With his own safety suddenly pushed to the back burner, Andy ran around the building toward Cabin 10's entrance...where The Figure had put a rather large hunting knife through the ginger head of Candice Travers, Victoria's childhood friend and fellow camp counselor. Not three feet from the shattered door to Cabin 10 and her friend's suddenly lifeless body, Victoria stood frozen in shock, her flashlight illuminating the carnage before her.

"Victoria!" Andy shouted. "Run!"

"Hey, Victoria!" Petey Waters shouted over the siren. "I'm gonna find out what the hell is going on. Stay with the kids."

"We're supposed to stay here, Petey-pie," Candice Travers reminded. "It's shelter in place, dumbass, not shelter wherever the hell you want to."

"She's right," Victoria told him. "Until we get the all-clear from Mr. Brannigan, we need to stay put."

"We still have kids out there, Vic," Petey argued. "Drew took his bunch out to pick blackberries and Dawn went for a run before picking her campers up at the craft lodge."

"They'll get to shelter," Victoria said. "This isn't their first rodeo."

"First or fifth," Petey said, "I ain't leaving anyone out there when I don't know what's got the sirens going. Plus, if we have a bear or a bobcat in the camp, Brannigan will shoot himself or one of our campers trying to get it. I don't trust that tubby coward to be running loose with a firearm."

"He's right," Victoria conceded. "Petey's the marksman. If someone is gonna play Hawkeye, I'd rather it be him."

"You saying I'm a superhero?" Petey asked, cocking one eyebrow.

"Wrong Hawkeye, dumbass," she replied. "I was talking The Last of the Mohicans."

"The Last of the—huh?"

"If you're going," Candice said, "get moving, Petey-pie. We've got to lock the door and get the kids calmed down."

"Wish me luck," he said, giving them a half-hearted salute.

"If you see Andy," Victoria started.

"Yeah?"

"Just...tell him to stay safe."

ONCE PETEY WAS GONE, CANDICE AND VICTORIA DID a quick headcount of rowdy campers who, for the time being, were wholly unaware of the bloody events happening elsewhere in camp. The count was one short.

"It's Dani," Lloyd Benton offered, while sword fighting Glen Hawkins with pipe cleaners stolen from the craft lodge. "She went to see that boy she likes from Cabin 7."

"Jeremy something-or-other," Lisa Gardner said, not bothering to look up from her book, a well-worn paperback copy of Ender's Game.

"Why didn't anyone say anything before?" Candice said.

"We don't snitch," Glen replied, slowly sliding to his imaginary death after being impaled on Lloyd's blue pipe cleaner.

"Lloyd did," Lisa reminded. "She's all hung up on him. I think they kissed last year. Or danced. Something she can't get over. It's dumb."

"I'm sure she's fine," Victoria whispered, "but I don't like not knowing what's happening."

"Brannigan's gonna have our asses for being a kid short," Candice said. "Might be our last summer pulling a paycheck."

"As long as everyone is safe," Victoria said.

"You say everyone," Candice chuckled, "but I think you mean Andy. Don't front, girl, you got it bad."

"I don't know what you mean."

"Okay. Sure."

"Candy—"

"He's cute," Candice said. "And he likes you, too. He gets that dumb grin on his face every time you talk to him."

"I think his smile is cute," Victoria replied. "And, yeah, I like him. But every time we have a chance for a moment alone, something comes up."

"I'll bet it does!"

Victoria punched her friend on the arm, then turned her attention back to Lloyd Benton, who she worried might put someone's eye out with his fuzzy weapon of choice.

JUST 10 MINUTES AFTER PETEY LEFT TO HUNT FOR stray campers and potentially procure a gun from Mr. Brannigan, who by that time was already long dead, the campers in Cabin 10 were quiet and wondering why the sirens were still blaring. They had gone through drills before, but this was clearly something different. Whatever was happening outside their walls was all too real.

"Petey-pie's gotta do something about that siren,"

Candice said, wincing. "It's putting my teeth on edge. And it's got the runts damn scared. First time they've been quiet in three weeks."

"I'm going to walk next door," Victoria said. "If Dani got caught in the storm, she may have gone back to our cabin, not knowing we were all sheltered here."

Candice nodded.

"Lock the door behind me," Victoria added.

"How will I know it's you?"

"Right," Victoria said, thinking about it. "I'll knock three knocks, three times."

"Sweet," Candice said. "And if you don't come back?"

Victoria hadn't considered that.

"I will," Victoria promised. "But if I can't, just stay hunkered down here until Brannigan gets to you. Or Petey. The important thing is that we keep the kids safe."

"Hey, wait," Candice said, turning back toward the campers. "Any of you kids sneak a phone into camp?"

They all looked up at her.

"No one will be in trouble," she promised. "If any of you brought a phone, now's the time to fess up. We need to call for help."

Sarah Till raised her hand. She was one of Victoria's charges from Cabin 11.

"My mom wouldn't let me come to camp unless I

promised to text her every day," she explained. "If I didn't sneak a phone in, I wouldn't get to stay."

"That's okay, sweetie," Victoria said. "Is it in our cabin?"

Sarah nodded.

"Under the mattress in my bunk," she said. "The code is 7-8-12."

"Thank you, love," Victoria said. "You guys sit tight and listen to Candice. I'm going to get us some help."

THE SOUND OF THE LOCK SOUNDED HAUNTINGLY final to Victoria as she stepped out into the pouring rain and walked the thirty muddy paces to Cabin 11. The dim cabin lights were cutting on and off thanks to the fury of the storm, giving the whole interior a bit of a strobe effect. She squeezed the water from her soaked t-shirt and grabbed her blue hoodie from her footlocker. It wouldn't do for all the pre-teen boys back in Cabin 10 to get their own wet t-shirt peek at their camp counselor.

She grabbed the flashlight that each cabin kept in their emergency kit and checked to make sure it worked. If they had to evacuate kids in the dark of night, she wanted to be prepared. She tucked the small first aid kit—essentially a box of bandages with a few packets of antiseptic ointment—into her hoodie pocket.

Sarah's phone was as easy to find as she had promised, and her passcode worked like a charm. Unfortunately, there was no reception. Victoria took a minute to write a simple text to 911 and hit send. Whenever the phone got a bar or two, it would send her request for help.

A lightning flash and crash of thunder made her turn her attention back toward the front door. The storm has grown in intensity until the siren, once piercing and headache-inducing, seemed somehow distant and weak.

"What a night," she mumbled to herself.

Another flash of lightning lit up the outside world, revealing a hulking silhouette walking past a window. The Figure seemed so unreal to her that the scream forming in her throat found no power to escape. Instead, she walked back to the front door as if in a dream. Her mind filled with a thousand realities, none of them pretty. If the threat wasn't a bear or a bobcat (as Petey had hoped), what sort of danger could be out there?

As she reached for the doorknob, her mind turned to Andy Vale. His smile. His laugh. His way with kids— sarcastic and biting to cover up his tenderness toward them. He was unlike anyone she had ever met, and she suddenly worried she'd never get to tell him so.

A loud crack, followed by the screams of children and splintering wood, shook Victoria from her stupor and returned her to the horrifying present. With a sudden rush of courage, she ran outside to see The Figure kicking the door into shards of MDF.

"Get away from them!" she screamed.

The Figure turned toward her, his blade catching the flickering porch light. Standing nearly seven feet tall and seemingly built of solid muscle, a rubber stag mask complete with antlers—bleached white by time in the sun or perhaps by some chemical concoction—covered its face. It turned toward her, its empty eyes sending a chill down her spine. It tilted its head as it considered her before taking a step toward her.

Victoria stepped back, and The Figure shortened the distance with another step. Behind him, Candice hurried the children out through the broken door and into the woods, running as fast as their young legs would carry them. If The Figure noticed their escape, it did not deter him from walking toward a terrified Victoria Adams.

"What do you want?" she asked.

The Figure brought its knife in front of his face and swiped the blood away, using two of its fingers as squeegees.

"Just leave us alone," she said. "I already called the cops. They're on their way."

The Figure took another step forward and Victoria stepped backwards, only to bump into the porch railing. She turned on the flashlight and shined it in The Figure's dead eyes. He remained unfazed.

"Leave her alone!" Candice shouted, hitting it with a cricket bat that had been Cabin 10 décor for more than a decade.

The Figure turned remarkably quick for something of its size, and seized Candice Travers by the throat, lifting her two feet off the muddy ground.

"Let her go," Victoria said, though the words came out so softly that the storm covered them completely.

But it was too late. With one move of its mighty arm, The Figure pierced the ginger-haired camp counselor through the forehead with its instrument of death exiting through the back of her skull.

Victoria screamed in horror, then heard Andy Vale shouting at her to run.

ANDY WAS SO GRATEFUL THAT VICTORIA SNAPPED OUT of her horror-induced stupor and ran toward the woods that it took him a moment to realize The Figure was now moving toward him. But something inside him, some instinct Andy was not consciously aware of, broke through his fear for the young woman he had grown so found of and prompted his legs to run.

The Figure's blade missed his throat by a fraction of an

inch as he broke around the killer to chase after Victoria. The only weapon in camp, aside from a few amateur hour bows and arrows, was the pistol in Brannigan's office. And Victoria was one of only two people with a key. If Pete was dead, her key was the only shot at ending the nightmare that had descended upon them like a plague.

As he cut between cabins 11 and 12, following Victoria's trajectory, he saw no sign of her on the path to the main office.

'Good girl,' he thought. 'Stay out of sight. Except, you know, I need the damn key, so...leave me a trail.'

He braved a glance back and saw The Figure following him. It made no effort to hurry. Why would death ever need to rush?

He felt the impulse to lead The Figure away from the office, as if some unseen hand was pushing him to get off the path and put his own survival ahead of the plan. Let Victoria go for the gun. Or better still, get the hell out of camp and put as much distance between himself and The Figure as possible.

'No,' Andy thought. 'I need the gun to save the kids.'

He got off the path and made a wide arc back toward Cabin 10, careful to make enough noise that The Figure might follow. He ran into an opening and stumbled over the dead body of Jasmine Pine, a 7th grade camper with a knack for giving people nicknames that stuck to them for weeks. The Figure had removed one of her arms and beaten her to death with it. The sight made Andy eject his lunch onto the grass beside her.

He heard the snap of a twig and rolled just out of reach of The Figure's bloody knife. Before he could recover, however, a second swipe of the blade cut through Andy's cargo shorts to bite into his thigh. It was a shallow cut, all things considered, but hurt enough that Andy's speedy retreat came with a limp. He had no doubt The Figure would follow.

'Too close,' Andy thought. 'One more mistake like that is all it will take. I need to get that gun.'

Cutting a serpentine path back toward Cabin 12, Andy's every instinct was to get back to the kids he'd locked in the mess hall pantry and head straight for the Hitchens' farm. But he wouldn't leave Victoria. Not with so many things unsaid. Ten yards or more to his right flank, he caught sight of The Figure moving silently through the foliage back toward the Red Path. He turned to continue his backtracking when moonlight glinting off an earring helped him spot Kenny Plimpton in his perch in the buckeye tree.

Kenny held his index finger to his lips.

Andy motioned for him to come down, but the frightened boy shook his head. Instead, he scribbled something on a memo pad he pulled from his pocket. Andy recognized it as one of the memo pads they always handed out to campers when they checked into camp. It encouraged the children to keep a journal of their experiences and friendships in camp. Most of the kids ignored the notion, but not little Kenny. He was a tender kid with the heart of a poet.

When the boy finished the message, he ripped it free of the pad, wadded it up, and dropped it down to the camp counselor whose name he didn't recall. The ink was running down the page, but Andy could still make it out. It read: Mr. Craig is behind the hydrangea bush.

Andy turned and saw a hand slowly wave from behind the large hydrangea bush three paces to his left. He ducked behind it to find Craig Shively on high alert, armed with a broken tree limb.

"That thing's close," Andy whispered. "How long have you and Kenny been hiding here?"

"Since that thing killed Jasmine," Craig said. His whole body was trembling, but not from the rain.

"I know hiding here feels safe," Andy whispered, "but it isn't. This thing killed Mr. B. And Candy. Pete, too. There's no safety until that thing is dead."

"Andy, I saw Hitchens fire a shotgun into that thing and it barely flinched," Craig whispered, shaking his head as if his memory was an Etch-a-Sketch and the movement might erase the horror. "He ripped his head free, Andy, and threw it at us."

"Old Man Hitchens was here?"

Craig nodded.

"Why? He hates this place."

"He said that thing killed his wife," Craig said. "Left a trail of her leading to the camp."

"The farm isn't safe," Andy mumbled.

"Didn't you hear what I said?" Craig whispered. "He blasted that thing with buckshot, and it didn't do shit. There's no killing it."

Andy's plan to rescue the children had centered on Brannigan's pistol. Without it, he needed a new plan.

'Run,' something inside him urged. 'Forget them all and run.'

"I need to find Victoria," he told Craig. "You should get Kenny out of here."

"Hell, no. That thing will find us," Craig said.

"You run that risk staying here," Andy argued. The fear he found in Craig's eyes softened his voice as he added, "but I understand. Stay safe. I'll come back for you once I find Victoria and the others."

Craig nodded, and Andy glanced back up at young Kenny Plimpton. The boy shook his head. He wasn't coming down from the tree.

There was no sign of The Figure as Andy Vale slowly made his way back alongside the Red Path. He wouldn't step out into the open or make any noise the storm wouldn't cover, but The Figure was still out there. He knew it was only a matter of time before he would come across it again.

Every instinct he had pleaded with him to flee, but

Andy continued to suppress the panic and fear, pushing it down into a little box somewhere in the back of his mind. Three things—and only three things—occupied his thoughts: Victoria, the kids, and killing The Figure.

Five yards from the office, while he still had the cover of the storm, the night, and the foliage, he moved around the perimeter. There were no signs of violence. No broken doors or windows. No lifeless husks of anyone Andy had once called a friend. If The Figure was near, he clearly hadn't found a convenient target.

He braved the open air long enough to sprint to the office door. He tried the knob and found it unlocked. Brannigan was dead. So was Pete. Only Victoria had the key.

'You assume,' his mind chided. 'You want so badly to play the hero; you aren't thinking straight. The girl could've given the key to someone else.'

He shook his head clear and pushed the door open, only to face the barrel of a snub-nosed pistol.

"Shit!" Victoria exclaimed, lowering the weapon. "I could've killed you."

"Seems to be on everyone's agenda tonight," Andy said, offering a smile. "That thing loaded?"

"Yeah," she said, handing it to him. "But I couldn't find any more ammunition. Six shots. That's it."

'It won't be enough,' he thought.

"It should...it should be enough," he lied. "Listen, Victoria, Petey is—"

He couldn't finish. She had known Peter Waters since they had been campers together as kids. He was the closest thing she had to an annoying kid brother. When he saw the tears trembling in her eyes, he stuck the gun in the pocket of his cargo shorts and embraced her. It was the first time he'd ever had his arms around her.

"You're hurt," she said, gripping him. "Your leg is bleeding."

"Nah," he said, reluctantly letting her go. "It's shallow. I got lucky."

"You saved my life," she said. "If you hadn't shouted and distracted him—"

"It's a life worth saving," he said, smiling bashfully.

"Where are your kids?" she asked.

"Safe. For now. But we need to put this thing in the ground, or we'll all be dead by dawn."

"You have a plan?" she asked hopefully.

"Step one," he offered, "stay alive."

"Check," she said.

"Get the kids to safety," he added. "And if The Figure gets in our way, put six in his brainpan so we can get the hell out of here."

She smiled at him awkwardly.

"What?" he asked.

"I think this is the most you've talked to me in three weeks," she said.

"Oh."

"No, I like it," she admitted. "I, uh, I like you, Andy. A lot. And I kind of suck at…I don't know…owning my feelings, I guess."

"Well, I'm great at it," he said with a chuckle. "I've wanted to ask you out since the day I met you and… well, you see how that panned out."

"Ask me," she said.

"Now?"

"Yeah. Now."

"Victoria, can I…would you let me take you to a movie sometime?"

"I'd love that," she said, kissing his cheek. "Just no horror movies."

"Agreed," he said. "I've had my fill."

"Then it's a date," she said. "Let's go save the kids."

He nodded and turned back toward the door.

"Keep the flashlight off and stay on my heels," he told her. "I'm gonna make sure the coast is—"

The machete came through the door with such force that it exited Andy's back before the young camp counselor even heard the splintering of the door. When The Figure pulled it free, Andy slid to the ground, his blood staining the pine floor as his vision grew dark.

Victoria's scream broke through his haze just enough for Andy to feel regret. The young woman he had grown so fond of would die...because he wasn't strong enough or smart enough to save her.

VICTORIA SPRINTED OFF THE RED PATH AND INTO the woods. After so many years at the camp, she knew them like the back of her hand. She wanted to get to the office, but staying on the path was a death sentence. She'd find another way.

Somewhere behind her, Andy Vale was dealing with the ramifications of distracting The Figure and buying her chance to escape...potentially with his own life.

'You can't go back,' she thought. 'Can't waste Andy's bravery. There are 134 kids in camp that need your help.'

The moment of Candy's death replayed in Victoria's mind on repeat. She could only assume Petey was dead, too. Who knew how many others? Whatever that thing was, it couldn't possibly be human. She had shined her light in its eyes and found no humanity. It was little more than a shape, a figure of death that would keep coming until they found a way to stop it.

'The gun,' she thought, remembering Brannigan's lecture about the responsibility that came with being given a key to the office.

"You need parent contact info, you come to me," he had told them, his gold chain and chest hair visible through his unbuttoned camp polo shirt, itself a size or two small. "I keep a gun in my desk in case we get bears sniffing around. Ain't happened yet, but I believe in being prepared. Anyway, the desk doesn't lock, so the office is always deadbolted. No opening it up unless there's an emergency and I'm not in camp."

'As emergencies go, Boss, this one's a biggie,' she thought.

She paused when she spotted The Figure stalking through the tall grass beyond the office. He was off the path and headed northwest toward the lake. She wasn't naïve enough to believe the threat was over, but his trajectory would take him far enough from the office that she would brave searching for that gun.

The pounding rain had long ago soaked through her favorite hoodie and the chill in the air would've had her shivering even if the carnage had not. She stepped out of cover and carefully made her way to the office, her head on a swivel for any sign of The Figure. The thunder would cover the sound of her feet on the porch, but the lightning made her feel on display, as if Mother Nature was shining a spotlight on her for The Figure to find.

The office door was locked. Fishing the key from the pocket of her denim shorts, she opened it, taking one last look behind to be sure she hadn't been spotted. Inside, she ignored the light switch to avoid calling attention to her presence and took a moment to let her eyes adjust to the darkness. The moonlight and the occasional burst of lightning would be enough illumination to find the gun.

For a moment, she wondered if Brannigan's living quarters above the office might contain a satellite phone or even an old school Ham Radio. Given Brannigan's greasy demeanor and the pervy way he always looked at Candy, she was pretty sure she didn't want to dig through his belongings. The gun was easy. She knew right where he kept it.

The bottom right drawer had a false bottom. Brannigan always joked that he had kept his coke stash there in the 80s. Now, it was home to a half-empty flask of cheap whiskey, a nearly full carton of no-filter cigarettes, Brannigan's 9mm pistol, and the loaded magazine you could hear rattling around every time he opened the drawer.

Carefully, she inserted the magazine into the grip, remembering the minimal instruction she'd received from her father, who believed everyone needed gun safety lessons even if they never planned to own one. She scanned a few of the other drawers for more ammunition, but found none. Twelve rounds would have to do.

She spent a few more minutes searching the office for anything that might be useful. She had hoped to at least find the machete Brannigan used to hack overgrown shrubs back from the footpaths around camp.

'He must've taken it with him,' she thought. 'Hell, if he's still alive out there, he might need it.'

Headed back toward the door, she paused when a lightning flash revealed the shadow of feet on the other side. Quietly removing the safety and chambering a round, she waited for a target, holding the gun the way her father had shown her two summers earlier.

The door swung open, and her finger tensed.

But it wasn't The Figure come to end her time at Camp Nightmare Lake.

It was Andy Vale. The boy she liked.

THE NIGHT HAD BEEN FILLED WITH HORROR. FROM watching her best friend skewered through the brain with a hunting knife to learning poor Petey-Pie—the nickname she and Candice had given him in 7th grade —had also met a grisly end, Victoria had never imagined she could feel so hopeless. But seeing Andy Vale skewered through the office door by The Figure mere seconds after finally asking her for a date, drove whatever hope remained inside her straight into an early grave.

She screamed his name. She couldn't help it. It was instinct. The shock of the moment put her on autopilot.

The Figure pushed through the door, his strength

brushing Andy's body aside as if it was weightless. The action left a swath of the young man's blood across the threshold. A flash of lightning illuminated the metal of the pistol gripped in the young man's now lifeless hand. The weapon was lost to her.

With soulless eyes, The Figure took her in, tilting its head as it considered her. Perhaps it was recognition. She had escaped him before.

Though part of her didn't want to leave Andy alone there on the pine floor of Brannigan's shabby office, her survival instincts took over and she turned to make use of the only other exit not currently inhabited by The Figure: the window behind the desk. She grabbed the computer monitor on the desk and hurled it through the glass, following it with a dive that her swimming coach would've chastised her for. She landed hard on the muddy ground outside, then struggled back to her feet.

She had no plan. She had no weapon. All she could do was run. And that she did.

For all of ten feet.

The Figure threw Brannigan's machete, still covered in Andy Vale's blood, with such force that it pierced the back of Victoria's left calf and split her tibia before breaking through the other side of her skin. She tumbled forward, screaming in pain, and doing irreparable damage.

As she cried and screamed, The Figure stepped off

the porch of the camp office and ambled toward her. The rack of its bleached buck mask caught every flash of light from the storm.

Victoria was Roman Catholic and, though she hadn't been to mass since her grandmother had passed away four years earlier, she still remembered her Our Father prayer. Through teeth clenched with pain, she whispered it as The Figure drew nearer. If what her grandmother had believed was true, perhaps the day would come when Victoria would see sweet Andy Vale again...and thank him for trying his best to save her.

As The Figure drew nearer, Victoria closed her eyes. She was scared enough without anticipating exactly how death would come for her. Instead, she focused on the prayer, and hoped that whatever horrors The Figure had perpetrated on the campers and counselors at Camp Montclair Lake, it would pay for them in eternity.

Then something happened that neither Victoria Adams nor The Figure could've expected. Lightning struck the camp office with such force that the building exploded as if it had been the target of a bomb. And in the middle of the wreckage stood a furious Andy Vale.

The Figure tilted its head and pulled its hunting knife—the same blade that had ended poor Candy—from the pocket of the gray coveralls it wore.

"You made a mistake," Andy said, his seeming to

come from everywhere around them. "You killed the wrong boy."

If The Figure understood words, it certainly seemed to give them no heed as he slowly trudged back toward the boy it thought it had already killed.

"I pleaded with him to run," Andy said. "I prompted, prodded, and manipulated his levels of anxiety, but Andy Vale wouldn't retreat. Oh, no. He had to make sure the loud, pimply children of this camp lived to see the bloody morning. And to see to it his precious Victoria would survive."

The Figure continued its slow approach. If it possessed thought, perhaps it wondered why the boy wasn't dead. Or perhaps, unlike poor Victoria, it understood that this new foe wasn't the same boy as the one it had stabbed through the office door.

"I was trapped, you see," Andy said, now hovering three feet above the wreckage of the camp office. "His body was my prison. For 17 years, I have been riding in the backseat of this boy's consciousness, rolling my eyes at his tenderness. At his loyalty. At his selflessness. I didn't even realize I cared for him until you started slaughtering his mates and the children he found such joy in."

A broken bit of pine, still on fire from the explosion, lifted into the air at the motion of Andy's left hand. His next motion split it into smaller shards and sent them flying forward, shredding The Figure's right knee and calf nearly down to the bone.

The Figure made no sound, but it stumbled and fell. It looked up at the boy, its masked face devoid of fear or any other emotion. As it struggled to stand, Andy continued.

"Over time, I suppose I came to admire Andy Vale," Andy said. "He reminded me of a friend taken from me too soon. We were at war then. For the fate of our world."

From her spot further down the path, Victoria could barely hear what was being said. The pain in her leg was so severe, she wondered if she was hallucinating this vision of Andy, floating in the air, his eyes seeming to glow with some verdant energy. When he wounded The Figure, she found a thread of hope again, clinging to the notion that somehow her prayer had been answered.

The Figure healed immediately upon his injury, his flesh and bone regenerating at incredible speed. It stood again and took another step toward Andy Vale.

"You reek of magic," Andy said to it. "And that will be the death of you. See, most every world they've imprisoned me in is devoid of the stuff. But here there's enough to turn myth into reality and the nightmares of children into flesh and blood terror. And where magic exists, devil, it is mine to command."

The wreckage of the office, from the burning 2x6s

of its framework to the paperclips from Brannigan's files, rose into the air on either side of Andy Vale, bullets in the chamber of a gun The Figure could neither see nor stop.

"You murdered the one person keeping me at bay," Andy said. "Worse still, you killed a boy I cared for. There will be no escape from my wrath. Your sentence is death. Pray that I do not follow you into hell to add to your torment."

A wave of Andy's hand sent the debris hurtling toward The Figure with such speed and force that it seemed like a second explosion. Like a swarm of locusts, the fragments of wood, metal, and plastic once contained in the office whirled around The Figure, chipping away at it until all that was left was a bloody smear diluted by the rain until it disappeared completely. Not enough left of it to regenerate. The Figure was no more.

Another wave of Andy's hand cause Victoria's pain to cease and she watched in awe as her bone and flesh were knit back together. A miracle.

As her summer crush floated her direction, descending slowly until he stood directly before her, she was still unsure of what was happening. Andy had gone from frightened camp counselor to flying super-hero after being impaled on what was essentially a garden tool. None of it made sense.

"You have questions," Andy said as he helped her

stand. "I'm afraid my answers will not bring you any peace."

"Andy?" she asked.

"No," he said. "Your Andy died when that creature stabbed him. And, with his death, I am free."

"You're a ghost?"

Andy scoffed.

"I'm a wizard," he said. "I know that makes no sense to you, girl. Your world differs greatly from mine. But there is magic here, and it helped create the monstrosity that spent the evening killing indiscriminately across this camp."

"Andy—"

"Azael," he corrected. "Andy is dead. I'm sorry. I know you cared for him."*

Though the things he said seemed impossible, Victoria believed him. So much so that she wept on his shoulder. The boy she liked was dead, and some wizard was wearing his body. The world had stopped making sense.

"You should know he cared for you," Azael said, his voice still Andy's, though with a hint of an accent she couldn't place. "You and those children were all he could think about."

---

* The wizard, Azael, often called "Azael the Sly" is a key player across the Evermore saga, playing out across Lemarr's other fiction.

"The children," she repeated. "You said they were safe, but I don't know where you...um, where, he—"

"They're locked in the mess hall pantry," he told her. "You'll find the key in a jar of flour. Brannigan is dead down by the boathouse. You'll need to contact the authorities. I'd leave the wizard out of the retelling, however, assuming you'd like to steer clear of the sanitarium. Let Andy be the hero. Tell them he died blowing that thing straight to hell."

"What about you?" She pushed back from him and discovered the eyes looking back at her didn't remind her of Andy at all.

"I've absorbed the magic that created the monster," he said, "but it's not enough to get me home."

"Where's home?"

He chuckled less at the question and more at the absurdity of trying to explain it to her.

"What was the game you and Andy played with your prepubescent charges last Thursday?" he asked.

"Castles and Clerics?"

"Yes," he said. "My world is a lot like that. Though with fewer minstrels and more pirates."

"Even after everything I saw tonight—" she started.

"It's a lot to take on faith, I know."

She sat down on a stump and the tears suddenly burst through her defenses, falling like rain even as the storm outside calmed. The wizard in her friend's body considered her for a moment, before kneeling before her.

"If you'd like," he offered, "I can wipe away your memory of Andy's death. The hard truth of it. Your last image of him needn't be painful."

She looked up at him with a question in her eyes, floating somewhere in the saline.

"To know that I am out there somewhere in his body will vex you, I'm afraid. Andy didn't really know I existed, but I...feel I owe him something of a debt. If I can serve you in this way—help you forget so you may heal—it would be my honor."

"But Andy—"

"Blew up the monster that killed so many campers and counselors tonight," Azael said. "He died a hero."

"He's really gone?"

Azael nodded.

"Then do it," she said. She closed her eyes and, when she opened them, remembered nothing after Andy Vale had blown himself and the killer up in the camp office. That and where she would find his frightened campers.

Camp Montclair Lake was closed for good and bulldozed to the ground the following summer. Camp Nightmare Lake was no more.

THIRTEEN WEEKS AFTER THE NATIONAL NEWS covered the strange story of a summer camp massacre perpetrated by an unknown drifter, Andy Vale—bearing new identification under the name Aaron Meridian—sat in a train station in Grimsby, Ontario, waiting for the train that would take him to New York City.

When the man approached him, he didn't bother to look up. He could feel him from the moment he entered the story, crackling with otherworldly power... but not the sort of magics Azael could bend to his will.

"Wearing the face of a dead hero isn't the smartest thing," the man said, taking a seat next to him. "Then again, hubris is one of your defining traits."

Azael turned and looked him over. His attire was appropriate enough for his surroundings, the collar of his navy pea coat turned up for just a hint of cloak and dagger. His tattoos, mostly hidden by his wardrobe, peeked out near the neck of his faded gray Henley.

"Considering an entire camp full of children decimated for lack of a hero, I don't think I'll take morality lessons from you, Darke. You and your protégé could've saved lives. Where was the Author of all stories that bloody night, hmm?"*

---

* Darke and his younger apprentice, Dylan Drake, work within the Evermore as agents of The Great Library at the behest of The Author. You can learn more about them and Azael in the FREE release, *The Willing, The Wounded, and The Wizard.*

Darke smiled and shook his head.

"You can't help it, can you? Missing the forest for the trees, I mean. Sometimes I think you're willfully blind to the Author's hand at work just so you can justify your rebellious inclinations," he said, turning in his seat to face the wizard. "Dylan and I weren't at the camp that night, Azael, because you were already there. You were the Author's provision. You were the help sent to save lives and end the threat of The Figure."

"I was a prisoner in some teenager's flesh and blood, Darke. I wasn't there willingly."

"No, you weren't. You were there because you were unjustly imprisoned across the Evermore. But the Author saw fit to use your misfortune for the good of those who survived. And, whether or not you see it, for your good, too."

"Please," Azael scoffed.

"Are you going to deny that Andy Vale left an impression on you? That his selflessness impacted the way you handled your freedom? You could've left those kids to deal with the monster on their own. Could've washed your hands of the whole thing and run."

"You think I'm a coward?"

"No," Darke admitted. "I think you're a selfish bastard who seldom puts the needs of others ahead of his own. But you did. You did what Andy had done prior to his death...put those poor kids first."

"He was a fool," Azael said. "Smart enough to have

scholarships waiting for him. He could've been someone. He could've cured cancer or solved the energy crisis. He could've mattered."

"Andy Vale did matter, Azael. Not for who he might have become, but for he was. Imperfect and fragile, sure, but full of grace and compassion."

Azael shifted in his seat, fighting the urge to scream.

"It wasn't fair," he said through clenched teeth. "He was decent and kind, and he didn't deserve to die."

"There's no such thing as fair, wizard. There's what is and what isn't. Andy Vale lived a predetermined number of days. They were his...to do with as he pleased. But they were up that night. Had he run, he'd have died without you being inspired to stand up in his place. He was a hero, Azael, and he inspired you to finish his good work."

The wizard took a deep breath and exhaled slowly.

"Are you here to take me home?" he asked.

"Is that what you want?" Darke asked.

"I have unfinished business to attend. Wrongs to set right."

"I agree," Darke said, "but this body can't travel with you there. You're only a fraction of yourself...a remnant of the whole. The moment of restoration will come in time, Azael. It was in motion before the Host imprisoned you. You'll need to be patient...which, as I recall, isn't your strong suit."

"Are you saying I'm stuck here?"

"Not exactly," Darke said, pulling a small book from the breast pocket of his jacket. He handed it to the wizard with a sly smile.

"What is this?" Azael asked.

"An assignment," Darke said. "A world with little hope where, while you await your restoration, you can still be a thorn in your enemy's side. It's only a door away if you're game."

"Who is this Margrave?" Azael said, flipping through the book.

"An enemy I inadvertently created," Darke admitted. "The Dark Queen planted him there to create an army of foot soldiers. You can disrupt all that. Their world needs a rebel. And, with your love of theatricality, I believe you'll inspire others to pick up where you leave off."*

"And if I decline?"

"You'll stay here until this very human body finally dies," Darke said. "Your magic can only prevent that for so long. When the end comes, you'll return to the Evermore, where you'll await restoration. This is an opportunity, wizard, not a forced relocation."

"You expect too much of me, Darke. I'm no hero."

"Are you sure? The children who escaped Camp

---

* The Margrave was first introduced in the horror collection *All That Waits in the Night.*

Nightmare Lake would disagree. It wasn't Andy Vale who ended their terror, Azael. That was you. Taking a stand against evil. You told me once—though I suppose from your side of events it hasn't happened yet—that we may never consider you a hero, but you've seen evil. You've seen what it can do. And you stand against it. Sometimes that's enough."

"What if I fail?" Azael asked, searching his eyes.

"You trust the Author has others that will see it done," Darke said. "I never know, Azael, whether each mission might be my last. But the Author is at work across worlds, timelines, and narratives, bringing hope to the hopeless and restoring what we've broken. Even if I don't live to see it finished, I believe our ending will be a good one. He will not leave your people to suffer."

"You make it sound easy," Azael said, shaking his head.

"No," Darke argued. "Trust is seldom easy. Faith is hard. Doubt quite simple. I know you think I'm a fool, but I've wrestled with doubt, Azael. That part of you is alive in me. Some days, I want to throw in the towel, retreat to my books, and escape to a place where the fight is finished. But He's given us this moment to act. To stand. I'm asking you to stand with us."

Azael closed the book and handed it back to Darke, who tucked it back into his pocket.

"Dr. Meridian, eh?" he asked. "Doesn't seem like a coincidence."*

"I know."

"Will you be there? I can't handle you being around all the time, looking over my shoulder."

"I'll help you get settled," Darke said, "then get out of your hair."

"The outfit seems fun."

"Definitely you," Darke agreed.

"Fine, then. Lead the way. Just don't expect too much of me."

Darke laughed at that, standing to lead the wizard to a doorway that would carry them to another world entirely.

"I never do, Azael," he admitted. "But you keep on surprising me."

---

* Azael has been known to use the alias, Dr. Meridien, in other tales, including his brief cameo in "The Cinder Man" collected in *Shadow Plays*.

ABOUT THE AUTHOR

photo by Shawn Cox

J. Patrick Lemarr lives in Indiana with his wife, Heidi, and their children. When he isn't crafting horror and fantasy, he is writing exclusive content for his Patreon supporters. Learn more at www.jpatricklemarr.com.

facebook.com/theofficialjpatricklemarr

patreon.com/jpatricklemarr

x.com/jpatricklemarr

instagram.com/jpatricklemarr

amazon.com/author/jpatricklemarr

threads.net/@jpatricklemarr

goodreads.com/jpatricklemarr

ALSO BY J. PATRICK LEMARR

Shadow Plays

All That Waits in the Night

The Christmas Cabin

The Willing, The Wounded, and The Wizard